Pooh
Invents a
New Game

A.A. Milne

Illustrated by E.H. Shepard

METHUEN

By the time it came to the edge of the Forest the stream had grown up, so that it was almost a river, and, being grown-up, it did not run and jump and sparkle along as it used to do when it was younger, but moved more slowly. For it knew now where it was going, and it said to itself, 'There is no hurry. We shall get there some day.' But all the little streams higher up in the Forest went this way and that, quickly, eagerly, having so much to find out before it was too late.

There was a broad track, almost as broad as a road, leading from the Outland to the Forest, but before it could come to the Forest, it had to cross this river. So, where it crossed, there was a wooden bridge, almost as broad as a road, with wooden rails on each side of it. Christopher Robin could just get his chin on to the top rail, if he wanted to, but it was more fun to stand on the bottom rail, so that he could lean right over,

 and watch the river slipping slowly away beneath him. Pooh could get his chin on to the bottom rail if he wanted to, but it was more fun to lie down and get his head under it, and watch the river slipping slowly away beneath him.

And this was the only way in which
Piglet and Roo could watch the river
at all, because they were too small to
reach the bottom rail. So they would
lie down and watch it . . . and it
slipped away very slowly, being in no
hurry to get there.

One day, when Pooh was walking
towards this bridge, he was trying to
make up a piece of poetry about
fir-cones, because there they were,
lying about on each side of him, and he

felt singy. So he picked a fir-cone up, and looked at it, and said to himself, 'This is a very good fir-cone, and something ought to rhyme to it.' But he couldn't think of anything. And then this came into his head suddenly:

♪ Here is a myst'ry
About a little fir-tree. ♩
Owl says it's his tree,
And Kanga says it's her tree.

'Which doesn't make sense,' said Pooh, 'because Kanga doesn't live in a tree.'

He had just come to the bridge; and not looking where he was going, he tripped over something, and the fir-cone jerked out of his paw into the river.

'Bother,' said Pooh, as it floated slowly under the bridge, and he went back to

get another fir-cone which had a
rhyme to it. But then he thought
that he would just look at the river
instead, because it was a peaceful sort
of day, so he lay down and looked at it,
and it slipped slowly away beneath
him . . . and suddenly, there was his
fir-cone slipping away too.

'That's funny,' said Pooh. 'I dropped
it on the other side,' said Pooh, 'and it
came out on this side! I wonder if it
would do it again?' And he went back

for some more fir-cones.

It did.

It kept on doing it.

Then he dropped two in at once, and leant over the bridge to see which of them would come out first; and one of them did; but as they were both the same size, he didn't know if it was the one which he wanted to win, or the other one. So the next time he dropped one big one and one little one, and the big one came out first, which was what he had said it would do, and the little one came out last, which was what he had said it would do, so he had won twice . . . and when he went home for tea, he had won thirty-six and lost twenty-eight, which meant that he was – that he had – well, you take twenty-eight from thirty-six, and *that's* what he was. Instead of the other way round.

And that was the beginning of the
game called

Poohsticks,

which Pooh invented, and which he and
his friends used to play on the edge of
the Forest. But they played with sticks
instead of fir-cones, because they were
easier to mark.

Now one day Pooh and Piglet and
Rabbit and Roo were all playing
Poohsticks together. They had dropped

their sticks in
when Rabbit
said 'Go!' and
then they had
hurried across
to the other
side of the bridge, and now they were
all leaning over the edge, waiting to see
whose stick would come out first. But it
was a long time coming, because the river
was very lazy that day, and hardly seemed
to mind if it didn't ever get there at all.

'I can see mine!' cried
Roo. 'No, I can't, it's
something else. Can
you see yours, Piglet?
I thought I could see
mine, but I couldn't. There it is! No,
it isn't. Can you see yours, Pooh?'

'No,' said Pooh.

 'I expect my stick's
stuck,' said Roo. 'Rabbit,
my stick's stuck. Is your
stick stuck, Piglet?'

'They always take longer than you think,' said Rabbit.

'How long do you *think* they'll take?' asked Roo.

'I can see yours, Piglet,' said Pooh suddenly.

'Mine's a sort of greyish one,' said Piglet, not daring to lean too far over in case he fell in.

'Yes, that's what I can see. It's coming over on to my side.'

Rabbit leant over further than ever,
looking for his and Roo wriggled up
and down, calling out 'Come on, stick!
Stick, stick, stick!' and Piglet got very
excited because his was the only one
which had been seen, and that meant
that he was winning.

'It's coming!' said Pooh.
'Are you *sure* it's mine?'
squeaked Piglet excitedly.
'Yes, because it's grey. A big grey one.
Here it comes! A very – big – grey—

Oh, no, it isn't, it's Eeyore.'

And out floated Eeyore.

'Eeyore!' cried everybody.

Looking very calm, very dignified, with his legs in the air, came Eeyore from beneath the bridge.

'It's Eeyore!' cried Roo,
terribly excited.

'Is that so?' said Eeyore,
getting caught up by a
little eddy, and turning
slowly round three
times. 'I wondered.'

'I didn't know you
were playing,' said Roo.

'I'm not,' said Eeyore.

'Eeyore, what *are* you
doing there?' said Rabbit.

'I'll give you three guesses, Rabbit. Digging holes in the ground? Wrong. Leaping from branch to branch of a young oak-tree? Wrong. Waiting for somebody to help me out of the river? Right. Give Rabbit time, and he'll always get the answer.'

'But, Eeyore,' said Pooh in distress, 'what can we – I mean, how shall we – do you think if we—'

'Yes,' said Eeyore. 'One of those would be just the thing. Thank you, Pooh.'

'He's going *round* and *round*,' said
Roo, much impressed.

'And why not?' said Eeyore coldly.

'I can swim too,' said Roo proudly.

'Not round and round,' said Eeyore.
'It's much more difficult. I didn't
want to come swimming at all today,'
he went on, revolving slowly. 'But if,
when in, I decide to practise a slight
circular movement from right to
left – or perhaps I should say,' he
added, as he got into another eddy,

'from left to right, just as it happens to occur to me, it is nobody's business but my own.'

There was a moment's silence while everybody thought.

'I've got a sort of idea,' said Pooh at last, 'but I don't suppose it's a very good one.'

'I don't suppose it is either,' said Eeyore.

'Go on, Pooh,' said Rabbit. 'Let's have it.'

'Well, if we all threw stones and things into the river on *one* side of Eeyore, the stones would make waves, and the waves would wash him to the other side.'

'That's a very good idea,' said Rabbit, and Pooh looked happy again.

'Very,' said Eeyore. 'When I want to be washed, Pooh, I'll let you know.'

'Supposing we hit him by mistake?' said Piglet anxiously.

'Or supposing you missed him by mistake,' said Eeyore. 'Think of all the possibilities, Piglet, before you settle down to enjoy yourselves.'

But Pooh had got the biggest stone he could carry, and was leaning over the bridge, holding it in his paws.

'I'm not throwing it, I'm dropping

it, Eeyore,' he explained. 'And then I can't miss – I mean I can't hit you. *Could* you stop turning round for a moment, because it muddles me rather?'

'No,' said Eeyore. 'I *like* turning round.'

Rabbit began to feel that it was time he took command.

'Now, Pooh,' he said, 'when I say
"Now!" you can drop it. Eeyore, when
I say "Now!" Pooh will drop his stone.'

'Thank you very much, Rabbit, but I
expect I shall know.'

'Are you ready, Pooh? Piglet, give
Pooh a little more room. Get back a bit
there, Roo. Are you ready?'

'No,' said Eeyore.

'Now!' said Rabbit.

Pooh dropped his stone. There was a

LOUD
splash,

and Eeyore disappeared . . .

It was an anxious moment for the watchers on the bridge. They looked and looked . . . and even the sight of

Piglet's stick coming out a little in front of Rabbit's didn't cheer them up as much as you would have expected. And then, just as Pooh was beginning to think that he must have chosen the wrong stone or the wrong river or the wrong day for his Idea, something grey showed for a moment by the river bank . . . and it got slowly bigger and bigger. . . and at last it was Eeyore coming out.

With a shout they rushed off the bridge, and pushed and pulled at him; and soon he was standing among them again on dry land.

'Oh, Eeyore, you *are* wet!' said Piglet, feeling him.

Eeyore shook himself, and asked somebody to explain to Piglet

what happened when you had been inside a river for quite a long time.

'Well done, Pooh,' said Rabbit kindly. 'That was a good idea of ours.'

'What was?' asked Eeyore.

'Hooshing you to the bank like that.'

'*Hooshing* me?' said Eeyore in surprise. 'Hooshing *me*? You didn't think I was *hooshed*, did you? I dived. Pooh dropped a large stone on me, and so as not to be struck heavily on the chest, I dived and swam to the bank.'

'You didn't really,' whispered Piglet to Pooh, so as to comfort him.

'I didn't *think* I did,' said Pooh anxiously.

'It's just Eeyore,' said Piglet. '*I* thought your Idea was a very good Idea.'

Pooh began to feel a little more comfortable, because when you are a Bear of Very Little Brain, and you Think of Things, you find sometimes that a Thing which seemed very Thingish inside you is quite

different when it gets out into the open
and has other people looking at it. And,
anyhow, Eeyore *was* in the river, and now
he *wasn't*, so he hadn't done any harm.

'How did you fall in, Eeyore?' asked
Rabbit, as he dried him with Piglet's
handkerchief.

'I didn't,' said Eeyore.

'But how—'

'I was BOUNCED,' said Eeyore.

'Oo,' said Roo excitedly, 'did
somebody push you?'

'Somebody BOUNCED me. I was just thinking by the side of the river – thinking, if any of you know what that means – when I received a loud

BOUNCE.'

'Oh, Eeyore!' said everybody.

'Are you sure you didn't slip?' asked Rabbit wisely.

'Of course I slipped. If you're standing
on the slippery bank of a river, and
somebody BOUNCES
you loudly from behind, you slip. What
did you think I did?'

'But who did it?' asked Roo.

Eeyore didn't answer.

'I expect it
was Tigger,'
said Piglet
nervously.

'But, Eeyore,' said Pooh, 'was it a Joke, or an Accident? I mean—'

'I didn't stop to ask, Pooh. Even at the very bottom of the river I didn't stop to say to myself, "*Is* this a Hearty Joke, or is it the Merest Accident?" I just floated to the surface, and said to myself, "It's wet." If you know what I mean.'

'And where was Tigger?' asked Rabbit.

Before Eeyore could answer, there was a loud noise behind them, and through the hedge came Tigger himself.

'Hallo, everybody,'
said Tigger cheerfully.

'Hallo, Tigger,' said
Roo.

Rabbit became very
important suddenly.

'Tigger,' he said solemnly, 'what
happened just now?'

'Just when?' said Tigger a little
uncomfortably.

'When you bounced Eeyore into the
river.'

'I didn't bounce him.'

'You bounced me,' said Eeyore gruffly.

'I didn't really. I had a cough, and I happened to be behind Eeyore, and I said

"Grrrr-oppp-ptschschschz."'

'Why?' said Rabbit, helping Piglet up, and dusting him. 'It's all right, Piglet.'

'It took me by surprise,' said Piglet nervously.

'That's what I call bouncing,' said Eeyore. 'Taking people by surprise.

Very unpleasant habit. I don't mind
Tigger being in the Forest,' he went on,
'because it's a large Forest, and there's
plenty of room to bounce in it. But I
don't see why he should come into *my*
little corner of it, and bounce there.
It isn't as if there was anything very
wonderful about my little corner. Of
course for people who like cold, wet,
ugly bits it *is* something rather special,
but otherwise it's just a corner, and if
anybody feels bouncy—'

'I didn't bounce, I coughed,' said
Tigger crossly.

'Bouncy or coffy, it's all the
same at the bottom of the river.'

'Well,' said Rabbit, 'all I can say is
– well, here's Christopher Robin, so *he*
can say it.'

Christopher Robin came down from
the Forest to the bridge, feeling all
sunny and careless, and just as if twice
nineteen didn't matter a bit, as it didn't
on such a happy afternoon, and he

thought that if he stood on the bottom
rail of the bridge, and leant over, and
watched the river slipping slowly away

beneath him, then he would suddenly
know everything that there was to be
known, and he would be able to tell
Pooh, who wasn't quite sure about some
of it. But when he got to the bridge and
saw all the animals there, then he knew
that it wasn't that kind of afternoon,
but the other kind, when you wanted
to *do* something.

'It's like this, Christopher Robin,'
began Rabbit. 'Tigger—'

'No, I didn't,' said Tigger.

'Well, anyhow, there I was,' said Eeyore.

'But I don't think he meant to,' said Pooh.

'He just *is* bouncy,' said Piglet, 'and he can't help it.'

'Try bouncing *me*, Tigger,' said Roo eagerly. 'Eeyore, Tigger's going to try *me*. Piglet, do you think—'

'Yes, yes,' said Rabbit, 'we don't all want to speak at once. The point is, what does Christopher Robin think about it?'

'All I did was I coughed,' said Tigger.

'He bounced,' said Eeyore.

'Well, I sort of boffed,'
said Tigger.

'Hush!' said Rabbit,
holding up his paw.
'What does Christopher
Robin think about it all? That's the point.'

'Well,' said Christopher Robin, not quite
sure what it was all about. '*I* think—'

'Yes?' said everybody.

'*I* think we all ought to play Poohsticks.'
So they did. And Eeyore, who had never

played it before, won more times than
anybody else; and Roo fell in twice, the
first time by accident and the second
time on purpose, because he suddenly
saw Kanga coming from the Forest,
and he knew he'd have to go to bed
anyhow. So then Rabbit said he'd go
with them; and Tigger and Eeyore went
off together, because Eeyore wanted to
tell Tigger How to Win at Poohsticks,
which you do by letting your stick
drop in a twitchy sort of way, if you

understand what I mean, Tigger; and
Christopher Robin and Pooh and Piglet
were left on the bridge by themselves.

For a long time they looked at the
river beneath them, saying nothing,
and the river said nothing too, for it
felt very quiet and peaceful on this
summer
afternoon.

'Tigger is all
right, *really*,' said
Piglet lazily.

'Of course he is,' said Christopher Robin.

'Everybody is *really*,' said Pooh. 'That's what *I* think,' said Pooh. 'But I don't suppose I'm right,' he said.

'Of course you are,' said Christopher Robin.

Pooh Invents a New Game
is taken from *The House at Pooh Corner*
originally published in
Great Britain 11 October 1928
by Methuen & Co. Ltd.
Text by A.A. Milne and line drawings by Ernest H. Shepard
copyright under the Berne Convention.

This edition published in Great Britain 2001
by Methuen Children's Books,
an imprint of Egmont Children's Books Limited,
a division of Egmont Holding Limited,
239 Kensington High Street, London W8 6SA.

3   5   7   9   10   8   6   4   2

Printed in China

ISBN 0 416 19957 7